How to Write a Bestselling Western Romance

Gallop your Way to the Hearts of Readers

Just Bae

Contents

Introduction

The Western romance genre has become widely popular for a few decades now, tapping into readers' nostalgia and escapism by transporting them to the late 1800s American frontier. With backdrops like the rugged countryside, small frontier towns, cattle ranches, and homesteads, novels in this genre embed adventure and passion into quintessential Old West settings.

Western romances draw heavily on American history while adding elaborate love stories to the mix. They resurrect the dangerous but wildly appealing world of cowboys, saloon brawls, cavalry soldiers, and Pioneer life on the Western plains with meticulously researched details. A few landmark titles that put frontier romances on the map are Lorraine Heath's Texas Destiny trilogy, beginning with 'Texas Destiny' (2011), and Rosanne Bittner's epic 'Savage Destiny' series, spanning seven books.

While set in the historical Old West, western romances feature strong, independent female protagonists who push norms and take matters into their own hands. Male leads also veer from stereotypes with moral ambiguity and emotional depth beneath a gruff cowboy exterior. These novels ride a line between authenticity and creative imagining of what roles women played as the frontier opened up.

Western romance took off in the 1980s and 1990s thanks to authors like Elizabeth Lowell, who blended action-packed plots with steamy tension in books like 'Only You' (1994). Around a decade later, the publishing category Romantic Westerns established some conventions: small-town settings, tensions between ranchers and homesteaders, and male protagonists being cowboys/lawmen/ranchers. Authors gave historical weight through Civil War references and native American characters while spotlighting progressive female characters and relationships.

The pace of life, remote, vast settings, and dangers of untamed frontier land made compelling backdrops for escapist heroic fantasies. Readers found themselves transported from mundane routines into epic survival quests, family vendettas simmering for generations, races to save a ranch from greedy land grabbers, etc. The solitary cowboy becoming enamored by the new schoolmarm is an oft-recurring plot, bringing personality clashes before true love wins out.

Western romance subgenres have expanded the possibilities: cowboy captivity narratives, westerns with paranormal elements, native American characters reclaiming narrative autonomy, and of course — forbidden interracial romances that upend social mores of the Frontier era. Many stories play on 'fish out of water' tropes, city-bred ladies adjusting to rural life adding to both comedic relief and central conflicts.

Steamy romantic scenes also thrive on the aura of rugged individualism and primal passions associated with cowboy mythos. Physical prowess is used to signal virility as much social machismo. Harlequin's line - 'Harlequin Historicals' and 'Harlequin Western Romance' have kept the flame burning for decades now updated with feistier heroines who confront alpha male leads, pushing back against female exploitation of lawless towns.

Western romances remain hugely popular today. In a 2020 poll of Nielson Book Research's dedicated romance fiction readers, Westerns were ranked the third most enjoyed subgenre behind contemporary romance and romantic suspense. On Goodreads, shelves like 'western-historical-romance are brimming with reader reviews. The compelling locales coupled with escapist adventure remain irresistible.

Ever-evolving subgenres point to new frontiers— sci-fi inflected Western romances like 'Through the Veil' by Colleen Halverson add paranormal magic and portals to pioneer America's historical reality. Kate Bateman's 'The Outlaw's Mail Order Bride' about a time-traveling modern woman saving a Bandit, brings action-movie badassery to tales set in the 1880s. The mythic West retains its hold over the reader's imagination even as historical accuracy expands diversely.(

So, aspiring authors know that the Western romance category has plenty of room for innovation and creativity alongside hitting genre conventions And building on romantic fantasies already proven to resonate with readers. Keep the adventurous pioneer spirit at the story's core! With gumption and grit, compelling characters, high-stakes drama, and burning forbidden passion— even a debut writer could wrangle herself a bestseller!

Chapter 1

Why Write a Western Love Story

You may wonder why you should consider writing a Western romance novel as an author looking to boost your readership. Consider the case made by the numbers—this genre has seen steady popularity over decades, suggesting a devoted fanbase always hungry for more. In Nielsen's 2020 romance reader survey, the Western historical subgenre came third in popularity after contemporary romance and romantic suspense.

Plus, the Western romance category is nowhere near saturation, suggesting you'll have an untapped market. Compared to long-established genres like mystery or thriller that see thousands of new titles annually. There's room to establish yourself as an auto-buy author. For instance, breakout success 'The Outlaw's Mail Order Bride' saw massive readership on Kindle Unlimited, indicating digital sales potential.

You can deliberately target various niche segments within the broad demographic attracted to Wild West settings and romantic plots ranging from loyal Harlequin imprint readers to young BookTok enthusiasts reviewing cowboy catnip titles on TikTok. Either way, quality writing that balances history and fantasy could make you the next household name.

Speaking of which, a sure-shot way to delight fans is by honoring classic Western tropes and flavor even within original storylines. Several recent bestsellers suggest these enduring plot devices—the arrogant rancher saved by the spunky sister-in-law, enemies-to-lovers reunited through danger, and the bandit seeking redemption for past misdeeds.

Think also of blockbuster references from recent years like Kristen Ashley's romantic suspense in 'Fairytale Come Alive' to Diana Palmer's passionate families in 'Wyoming Brave' and look at reader reviews on what made them compulsively readable page-turners. Build on those core strengths.

Having an eye on successful predecessors helps strategize what new angles to bring to Western romance so you stand apart. Study reader reviews and see which emotional strings aren't being tugged enough. Do loyal readers want more stories about cowgirls or non-white characters instead of the typical cowboy lead? Should sex scenes get steamier?

Is there an appetite for grittier, more textured backstories or conflicts beyond a ruthless land grabber destroying honest, hardworking Ranchers? The variety says readers crave both historical authenticity and also more inclusion, going beyond stereotypes. Delivering that could make your book a critical and commercial success.

Besides hitting genre hallmarks like the gruff cowboy hero winning over the feisty heroine, tap broader 2022 reading trends absorbed from genres beyond westerns a la Kennedy Fox's 'Tycoon' cowboy incorporating a moody billionaire trope. Blend tried-and-tested fantasy elements that convert casual romance fans into die-hard believers demanding book two the moment they finish your irresistible novel of passion and gunslingers.

Maintain the escapism, letting weary today's readers vividly imagine themselves on vast Frontier plains, rugged landscapes dotted by mines, ghost towns, and saloons with swinging doors frequented by mysterious dangerous Strangers you introduced wearing historically accurate hats. Describe that world through precise sensory details. Brand yourself a leader staking new territory in Western romance gold country.

Ultimately, you have artistic control over crafting characters and conflicts that steer expectations into surprising directions through the inherent thrill and adventurous Spirit of Westerns. Embrace this world-building potential for blockbuster bookshelf potential based on reader enthusiasm. When it comes to Western romance, the advice is simple: You'll regret not saddling up for this rewarding writing ride sooner!

Chapter 2

Your Audience

When gearing up to write in the Western romance category, it's crucial to understand just who your book will land in front of. The good news is that readers of frontier-set historical romances represent a sizable, devoted demographic. Overlap greatly exists across general romance fiction readers, as per industry data.

Specifically, Nielsen Book Research's 2020 report studying romance fiction readership provides useful insights. Of respondents actively choosing Western romances as a preferred subgenre, 82% fell between ages 30 to 60. The majority (60%) were aged 40 and above. Life experience plays a role - perhaps reminiscing fond memories of 1970s-80s Hollywood Westerns from youth!

Just over half this Western romance readership lived in suburban areas, while almost 20% hailed from rural country locales, perhaps finding the ranch setting & countryside comforting escapism from hectic urban life. 60% had above-average household incomes, suggesting higher spending power for hardcover purchases.

It's important to note that the Western romance readership is overwhelmingly women - 96% identifying as female readers. This indicates a strongly gendered target audience. While diversifying representation is worthwhile, it's crucial to focus on writing heroines with insightful nuance about their ambitions, identities, and inner lives. This aligns with the readers' preference for strong female characters.

Goodreads community reviews provide added texture, showing just what readers prioritize. Sense of adventure, tension between desire and propriety, and a resonant coming-of-age journey rank highly. Fans emphasize lead couples who meaningfully impact each other's arcs. Authentic dialogue avoiding modern speech patterns also adds immersion.

Notable is the appeal of strong-willed female protagonists bucking social conventions - teaching, doctoring, and running businesses independent of male approval in the Frontier era. Heroines written as fighters and survivors connect, although heartfelt emotion with love interests takes priority over anything too gritty. Accessible writing is preferred over literary pretense.

Another marketing study by iResearch in China interestingly found urban professional women were emerging fans. Over 52% held university degrees and above. The foreign cowboy archetype and idea of a free, liberating landscape captivated restless minds in high-stress environments. This brings global opportunities.

In conclusion - female readers aged 30 to 60 years old comprise your core target audience with personal appreciation for both escapism and feminine empowerment in a vivid historical setting. Know their preferences through actual reading patterns vs hypothesizing! Write books speaking directly to women, much like the daring heroines found between the pages.

Chapter 3

Knowing the Western Genre

A common question aspiring authors face is - how does my novel qualify specifically as a Western romance vs. encroaching on other Western genres? While the pictorial small-town Americana settings may overlap, the themes and plots differ. Western romance primarily centers on romantic development between lead protagonists, while subgenres like Western thrillers pivot the external peril they face.

The classic Western usually features a lone cowboy anti-hero in the style of John Wayne who saves locals from villain bandits through quick wits and marksmanship. Romantic elements take a backseat to adventure-driven plots. Zane Grey's frontier novels like Riders of the Purple Sage epitomized dramatic action spectacle, which later gave rise to Western movies and TV shows.

Compare this to heartfelt tales in Western romance, putting the love story first. Any action occurs in service of bringing soulmates together or tearing them apart with emotional resonance. Settings facilitate intimacy between leads. While external conflict peppers in drama, romantic arcs evolve the central relationship.

Western Historicals constitute another intersecting circle on the genre Venn diagram. These recreate the pioneer era in extensive detail from fashion, customs, speech patterns, and social dynamics, but romantic plots aren't the principal focus. Religion, survival quests, and territorial disputes occupy narrative attention instead of romantic chemistry between leads.

Western thrillers take historical landscape and archetypal cowboy hats, then fuse with high-stakes suspense, mystery, and visceral action similar to modern crime fiction. C.J. Box's Joe Pickett novels add environmental twists to frontier justice and detection through a Wyoming game warden protagonist. These hybrids leverage Wild West's legacy as a versatile canvas for the imagination.

Westerns also see shades of science fiction, steampunk, paranormal, and more. Steampunk incorporates retro-futuristic technology, creating alternate frontiers with cyborgs, airships, and Victorian cowboys. Space cowboys in space chasing intergalactic bandits and extraterrestrial threats. Flexibility allows extensive creative license through hybridization while upholding genre roots.

More mainstream Westerns tend to be plot-driven, using stereotyped characters, while romance-centric stories feature more nuanced introspection into identities, social limitations, and second chances. Emotional satisfaction triumphs over suspending disbelief regarding a happy ending. Reader projections manifest through the heroines written with independence, eschewing traditional motherhood.

Common ground does exist between Western subgenres, however - the iconic visual imagery rooted in cowboy culture, concentration on personal grit, overcoming life-threatening challenges, and the stark contrast of rugged individualism against communal bonds. The distinct flavor comes from selectively heightening some ingredients over others to craft tonally different reading experiences tapping the same cultural history.

In Western romances, delicious tension simmers between leads in tentative courtships, timidly navigating strict Frontier-era relationship conventions before shared ordeals dissolve pretense, allowing vulnerability, interdependence, and, ultimately, marriage. Separate subplots like a cattle empire sabotage may loom large but function as a catalyst for confessed feelings.

Compare this to a Western thriller zeroing in on the sabotage itself with a protagonist single-mindedly hunting the perpetrator with detective laser focus and cool rationality. Any romantic angles feel incidental to cracking the investigation. Here, the role is not to have a love interest that defines character stakes. Readers thrill-seeking mystery, revelation, and justice above melting into a compassionate kiss.

In plain terms, this genre of romance dwells on affairs of the heart with wished fulfillment while subgenres like Westerns, Western Histories, etc. explore affairs of a world where day-to-day existence a heavier burden characters bear with stoic trailblazing spirit carving out communities against harsh, beautiful frontier terrain; camaraderie more symbolic than solace found in a paramour's arms. Choose priorities accordingly!

Nonetheless skillful storytelling should generate affection for protagonists from sundry subgenres so readers invested in their welfare. Inject earnest charm and charisma to give cool; calculated cowboy archetypes magnetism on par with the passionate smolder emanating from Western romance leads.

Ultimately, all trails lead back to the majestic Wild Frontier outlaw ideology, letting individuals determinedly chart their own path, which charms readership. Embellish beloved touchstones but focus thematically convey distinct flavor, be it swoon-worthy Harlequins or brooding Louis L'Amours. Mastering the keynotes and instrumentation choices is important to hit the right chord with audiences in this diverse genre bounty.

Chapter 4

Establishing the Theme – Pt. 1

Transporting readers to the late 19th-century American frontier requires vividly recreated settings that feel like stepping into a dusty time machine. Historical authenticity in architecture, terrain, flora, and fauna establishes believ-ability so readers are immersed in frontier life. So, saloon swing doors should creak the right way, sagebrush and tumbleweeds populate desert plains and log cabins should be brought to life through hard labor and tools of the 1800s.

Iconic Western locales like a sprawling cattle ranch, rustic village main street, and threadbare one-room schoolhouse surrounded by miles of empty landscape instantly trigger keen nostalgia for 'the good ole days' suggesting simpler times, wholesome values, gritty self-sufficiency contrasted with mod cons. Leverage this wistfulness but sharpen backdrops until readers taste trail dust.

Homesteads and ranches form the backbone of Western romance settings strongly associated with agrarian existence – farmlands, livestock, timber mills, etc. along with amenities township communities create through collaboration supporting families bonded by geography and culture. Frontier settlers' transportation relied on horses before railroads expanded access from east to west. Makeshift blacksmith sheds and trading posts sprang up, catering to needs in relative isolation.

Rugged untamed topography proves alluring with an ambiance uniquely 'Western', whether mountains, valleys, buttes, or wide plains where the sky feels endless. Have openings establish scope and signatures - desert heatwaves, Glacier lakes, vegetal choked waterways, etc. elaborating on textures and palette conveying scale before zeroing in on the ranch house front porch.

Small frontier towns are also quintessential cultural touchstones in the genre, where scattered buildings clustered on a windswept plain with horses tied up on railings and locals gathering to trade gossip. Recreate ornate saloons with swinging doors, general stores, an expanding railway station, schoolhouses, straw-roofed barns, Apothecary displaying cured meats behind glass jars, and little laundry cottages belching coal smoke.

Edifices served functions dictated by the environment and social dynamics before sophistication, so rough-hewn log cabins caulked with mud, lean-tos sheltering handfuls of livestock through bitter winters, stonewalls drawing groundwater - buildings crafted through callused hands blistered by splinters and determination compared to modern modular construction. Honor cultural memory by resurrecting this history.

Language communicating hardship the pioneers stoically endured still profoundly stirs readers when well-chosen signifiers establish capacities tested by extreme conditions - a three-day ride to collect provisions in the nearest township, fireside chats under starlight skies musing over genealogy, boiling coffee grounds twice to stretch rations. Such hardships are now exotic to contemporary culture lived daily.

Beyond recurring visual cues, creative descriptions spotlighting signature technology tools and equipment used back then also cement historical setting - muskets and powder kegs giving way to sharper revolvers, months dedicated to quilting bees stitching blankets to protect against the elements, hunting by lantern light tracking dinner, physicians sterilizing instruments over a flame.

Readers long fed by Hollywood myths also have an expanded appetite for greater authenticity rather than recycling fables of white male cowboy machoness saving damsels and towns single-handedly.

For a sense of progress measured through the ages rendered in buildings, catalog arriving innovations altering ways of life gradually: telegraph wires stitched across plains, saloons acquiring pianos, schoolhouses expanding into colleges, ranches acquiring agricultural technology, etc. Contrast old-fashioned methods with modernization, showing time passage.

Importantly, integration into plots should always highlight human stories - how do characters meaningfully interact with their habitat and relate to resembling their resilience or vulnerability? Does terrain pose specific challenges overcome through grit? Do they reminisce about childhoods once full of promise before tragedy reduced their dwelling into disrepair?

Think also seasons beyond broad strokes about winter freezes and summer droughts. How does torrential spring rainfall flood crops, core reader catnip, and the smoldering build-up between romantic leads often uses metaphoric weather - thunderstorms sparking electricity foreshadowing suppressed desire soon to be unleashed by a passionate downpour!

Move closely with characters charting how habitats evolve relationships with natural order and community. Do falling Autumn leaves mirror fading optimism about the future? Are they spurred by competitive streaks to prove naysayers wrongs prediction they would fail as pioneer settlers? Perhaps Spring coupled with a newborn foal restores courage after personal storms.

Moments resonating most fondly over time become folkloric memories slotted into personal mythologies that underscore regional identities even today. Render micro seasons in pointillist detail, too - the bittersweet harvest marking the closure of another year's graft, county fairs commemorating unity despite families living miles between, even minor snowstorms becoming landmark township calendar events kids reminisce about as adults.

And side characters should populate the landscape too, bringing distinctive charm - traveling musicians wandering into makeshift saloon concerts, the village pastor making his way between scattered homes, a traveling photographer documenting monumental migrations only ever witnessed by wild buffalo before, the occasional visit by indigenous tribes signaling rainfall portents ahead.

By getting granular, authors steward whole universes familiar yet captivatingly exotic that satisfy escapist yearnings. Settings loosely inspired by history but endowed lovingly with symbolism, letting protagonists discover revelations about themselves reflected through the land around them readers traverse eagerly live vicariously. Then, in closing chapters, they may sigh farewells, bidding goodbye to touchstones, making this Western microcosm feel more genuinely 'home' than where they actually reside!

Chapter 5

Establishing the Theme – Pt. 2

When writing Western romances evoking bygone eras or contemporary times, immerse readers in vivid atmospheres epitomizing rugged individualism, raw grit, and unbreakable loyalty forged through shared hardships. These enduring core values of frontier living still captivate modern imaginations seeking connection to simpler times, prioritizing honor and resilience over superficiality.

Transport audiences convincingly by conveying period-specific daily challenges your characters navigate that galvanize bonds. In "Rosanne Bittner's Outlaw Hearts series," Jake risks life and limb pursuing vigilante justice after society fails him while simultaneously tenderly wooing Randy. Their romantic arc feels earned because you viscerally understand the dangerous work and moral codes compelling them together as partners against corruption.

Similarly, it spotlights how unforgiving natural landscapes shape psyches and livelihoods. "Beverly Jenkins' Tempest" captures arid Arizona heat waves and torrential downpours mirroring the tempestuous attraction between horse breeder Rhine and reporter Rosie as they clash and then unite to build her family ranch. Appreciation for nature's brutality and beauty reflects the pioneering spirit itself.

While Old West perils like lawlessness and skirmishes with indigenous tribes recur frequently in classic historicals, look beyond shopworn stereotypes. "Kristin Hannah's The Great Alone" refreshingly depicts 1970s Alaska homesteaders battling PTSD and domestic abuse when Vietnam vet Ernt transplants his wife and daughter into remote wilderness. You empathize with women's harrowing limited options in eras of #MeToo progress.

So, when creating Western heroines, celebrate feminine gumption through three-dimensional inner lives rather than reactive damsels or Pollyanas. In "Jodi Thomas' Ransom Canyon", Staten grapples over selling her inherited Texas acres amidst the 1890s drought before Dan revives her passions. You see economic autonomy's importance and romantic fulfillment's mutual healing, defying reductive stereotypes.

This applies doubly portraying indigenous experiences. Transcend tokenism with nuanced backstories honoring specific tribal ancestry without cultural appropriation.

"Beverly Jenkins' Night Hawk" introduces sharp-shooting Civil War veteran Ian Vance, who happens to be Comanche, rather than employing heritage one-dimensionally. You relate to his resilient humor overcoming prejudices just like his Irish beloved Maggie.

Regardless of time periods, environmental threats perpetually plague ranchers and farmers. Make capricious weather symbolic challenges your couple braves together like Dorothy Garlock's Westermoreland Trilogy heroes nurturing love through bleak American Dust Bowl poverty and infertility mirroring barren 1930s Kansas soil. Descriptive details immerse you in harsh realities, magnifying emotional journeys.

Take cues from Bestsellers like "Linda Lael Miller's Stone Creek novellas" introducing quirky small towns where everybody nose neighbors' affairs gossiping over morning coffee. Eccentric supporting casts provide grounding humor, counterbalancing melodrama organically. You cherish community closeness vicariously through little anecdotes revealing interdependence's daily texture.

Authenticity arises by layering historical ambiances with meticulous research – wardrobe, diction, decor, and behavioral mores delineate eras unobtrusively. In Jo Goodman's Copper Beach, Shea's corsets and Mason's cavalry mannerisms breathe life into 1880s coastal Maine harbor naturally rather than belabored exposition. You get engrossed because Goodman prioritizes character-driven storytelling over didacticism.

Conversely, contemporary Westerns allow creative license updating hallmarks for modern audiences. Lorelei James' Rough Riders erotica openly celebrates rancher kink predilections flouting Old West puritanical repressions. You titillate imagining how Brody's dominance liberates poised Natalie's uninhibited urges amidst recognizable 21st-century North Dakota backdrops.

Yet traditional Western literary tenets like rugged masculinity and distressed damsels warrant thoughtful examination in post #MeToo landscapes. "Victoria Dahl's contemporary Copper Ridge" series still retains beloved tropes, but her city slicker Zane initially underestimates Wrangler Sierra's competence before respecting her self-reliance. You swoon harder because their HEA feels progressively earned through humbling self-awareness, not sexism.

So remember, Western romance iconography supplies adaptable narrative bones you can flesh with diverse perspectives across generations. In LaVryle Spencer's Morning Glory, Will's 1940s chivalry first clashes with Elly's Great Depression resourcefulness, but their grudging teamwork blossoms into appreciation emblematic of their respective resilience. You root for them as people, not just archetypes.

Beyond just page-turning plots, endow multi-faceted casts with timeless motivations resonating across divides – Alyssa Cole's An Extraordinary Union merges Americana adventure with interracial passion undermining slavery between Elle's spy prowess and Malcolm's military gallantry. You swoon harder because forbidden yearning surmounts societal restrictions reinforcing universal humanity.

Ground circumstances reinforcing frontier communities' insularity, too, like Sarah MacLean's Lonesome Dove saga descendants, still begrudging past feuds derailing young love until catastrophes supersede grudges. You empathize because similar petty grievances sabotage real-life reconciliations until a crisis reveals what truly matters. Specific dynamics echo human truths.

But balance gritty warts-and-all realism with uplifting hopefulness – Pam Crooks' Hannah's Vow heroine rebuilds life after her outlaw husband's crimes, but forgiveness remains elusive until childhood friend Seth embodies second chances. You believe her guarded transformation from bitterness into redemptive love because Crooks captures grace's authentic struggle.

For escapist historical romances, evoke ambiances free from modern cynicism that still feel relatable. Jude Deveraux's Knight in Shining Armor plucks 1990s Dougless into 1560s England, where Nicholas' unwavering devotion heals her self-esteem. You vicariously bask in their fantastical bond's purity despite knowing rationally chivalry's fallibility. Deveraux's sincerity stirs old-fashioned romantic faith.

In contemporary settings, mine modern career pressures and dating mores for fresh conflicts and comic relief. Jennifer Crusie's Getting Rid of Bradley contrasts Kensington Press cutthroat with unassuming Kyle's steadfast decency after cheating fiancé returns. You laugh knowingly about toxic ex-drama and cubicle politics before sighing contentedly when nice guys finish first.

Similarly, Jill Shalvis' Animal Magnetism series proves tender-hearted tough guys wielding puppies and kittens melt secret softies' reservations faster than macho flexing. You grin at Adam, wooing cold Holly through goofy pet antics alongside smoldering glances. Playful humor complements steam, mirroring well-rounded love's give-and-take.

Immersive accuracy ultimately matters less than meaningful characterizations. Courtney Milan's historical Brothers Sinister saga anachronistically spotlights bluestocking Violet's astronomy passion based on scant period female scientists. Yet you admire Violet's uncompromising ambitions when Sebastian respects her intellect and desire equally. Their central dynamic's substance trumps cosmetic details alone.

Chapter 6

Your Characters from Cowboy to Heroine

Western romances build intrigue and nostalgia by reinventing iconic character types from America's frontier era. The stoic cowboy ethos encapsulated by the mysterious brooding rancher or fierce but moral outlaw remains catnip. Fans swoon over alpha tendencies balanced with glimpses of vulnerability when the love interest chips away their stone-cold facade.

Lucian West in Kennedy Fox's contemporary 'Tycoon' fits the gorgeous billionaire cowboy trope to a T with luxury ranches and a ruthless tycoon reputation. But his instant attraction to heroine Paige softens his demeanor into protectiveness and scorching passion. This theme recurs in Diana Palmer's 'Wyoming Tough' where protector cowboy Bragg has walls from past hurt until Bess's innocence disarms him.

Complementing the macho cowboy is the gutsy, sharp-tongued heroine unwilling to be dominated or patronized. She stands her ground firmly despite social odds stacked against lone pioneer women. Her defiance thinly veils courageous integrity, and the stone-faced cowboy cannot help but admire once-past irritation.

In Lorraine Heath's classic 'Texas Destiny', headstrong Houston weds Dagmar then must convince his unwilling bride their marriage can work. Dagmar distrusts men, but Houston's humor and respect thaw her misgivings. Joan Johnston's 'Wyoming Bride' has cattle heiress Jessy Wentworth reject suitor Creighton to prove herself running her father's ranch before acknowledging their electric chemistry.

Beyond lead couple tropes, western romances populate the backdrop with era archetypes. Saloon dancing girls that catch cowboys' eyes, corrupt land officials scheming against honest ranchers, Native American tribes fighting encroachment on sacred lands, even plucky orphan side-kicks who befriend protagonists.

Characters may start out stereotypical before deeper dimensions emerge - the humble preacher hiding trauma from the civil war, the cosseted society lady defying her family by becoming a frontier doctor, and thence, who secretly sympathizes more with Native tribes than white settlers. Nuance supersedes cliches.

Some secondary characters epitomize comic relief- the garrulous ranch cook prone to gossip, the bumbling deputy more interested in fishing than law enforcement, and the eccentric old-timer whose tall tales about adventures contradict his age. Lightness offsets heavy themes.

Villains also have archetypes- the violent bandits terrorizing towns, the wealthy tycoon ruthlessly seeking to dominate all cattle ranches, crooked sheriffs abusing authority to commandeer homesteads, etc. Backstories explaining their malicious motivations make them chilling rather than cartoonish.

Whatever the archetype, protagonists confront challenges highlighting grit and integrity with high stakes. Something about the sparse, brutal frontier existence distills characters to their essence. Protagonists written as fighters more than lovers may thrive in Western thrillers instead of romance.

While archetypes draw readers in with familiarity, originality comes from twisting expectations. A bandit could be avenging a great injustice; the soft-spoken ranch hand secretly writes poetry. Archetypes are skeletons that have compelling backstories, motivations, and flaws flesh out.

References to actual historical figures like Annie Oakley, Buffalo Bill, Sitting Bull, etc, enhance resonance for readers fondest for the era. Famous names feel comforting, akin to celebrity cameos versus wholly fictional characters. Grounding in actual Old West people and events taps collective nostalgia.

In conclusion, incorporate character archetypes as creative launchpads but subvert stereotypes through emotional depth and surprising backstories. The taciturn sheriff could secretly write maudlin country tunes; the prissy hypotheses has deadshot aim with a hunting rifle. Use tropes, then twist sharply!

Flaws, Backstories, and Motivations

Flawed, yet dimensional and relatable characters, are the lifeblood of standout Western romance fiction. These characters, despite living in historic settings, have the power to draw readers in. The key to their allure lies in their imperfections, their flawed nature. Their backstories and motivations, far from being perfect, add texture, empathy, and room for personal growth as the romantic journey unfolds.

The most compelling protagonists are not moral paragons, but individuals who grapple with their own shortcomings and past traumas. These past wounds, both physical and emotional, shape their character and their journey towards redemption. Childhood grief, wartime PTSD, vengeance sought against those who wrongfully harmed loved ones in the past - these are the scars that make these heroes fascinating leads.

These past wounds, both physically scarred and psychically haunting, make taciturn cowboys perfect foils for sunny, optimistic heroines who encourage them to process buried pain. Their non-judgmental patience erodes walls, allowing a softer side hidden by machismo gruffness to emerge, made visible through glimpses of nurturing protectiveness towards the heroine and those dependent on the cowboy.

Equally poignant are the heroines, who, despite societal limitations, strive to overcome their past and find love. These fiercely independent women often harbor secret fears of romance, yet they crave loving reciprocation. Their journey is not easy, but with the patience wooing from empathetic male protagonists who respect their boundaries, they find the strength to heal and grow. This subtle courtship dance, underpinned by mutual care, helps both parties heal collectively.

Side characters beyond the central couple also shine brighter when written insightfully as more than stereotypes. The villain seeking violent revenge could have understandably suffered greatly once, the preacher's wife dutifully battling private alcoholism, or the noble Native tribal chief concealing health issues while guiding their community - backstories eliciting empathy, even for morally questionable folks, add depth.

Another hallmark of converting stereotypical frontier Western characters into unforgettable breakouts is crafting strong motivations and aspirations beyond expected gendered conventions. Defiance transforms emotions into purposeful action.

The saloon singer making money long-term to fund her own business, the courageous lady blacksmith secretly repairs tools better than any male competitor while facing social stigma, the wrongfully widowed teacher who funds her own school to educate local urchins left behind by settlers heading West - historically grounded motivations conveying ambition and self-defined success resonant amazingly well with readers even centuries later by subverting gender norms of the 1800s.

Even mundane goals become compelling when achievement seems unsure, and viewers deeply invested: will the couple save enough to buy their own plot of ranch land? Can the estranged siblings rebuild their family homestead left abandoned after smallpox tragedy? Stakes feel higher when protagonists are clearly underdogs overcoming internal demons and external threats.

Romantic Chemistry

Romantic tension simmering between your protagonists should sweep readers up into a will-they-won't-they frenzy as irresistible attraction battles propriety and danger. Masterful storytelling has audiences invested in each longing glance and casual touch that betrays suppressed desire between the fiercely independent cowgirl and brooding ranch owner she's strangely drawn to despite their differences.

The key lies in building multiple story layers, establishing them as kindred spirits beneath outward projection. What values or personality traits make them compatible despite class/status divides of the historical frontier setting? Shared mourning of a mentor, mutual loneliness seeking kinship, admiration for each other's survival skills when thrust together battling threats in the unforgiving land-scape – fertile groundwork strengthens bonds.

Next, create moments subtly revealing admiring glimpses beneath the facade that only readers notice initially. Maybe the cautious ingenue watches the confident roper stride back from the stables with a flicker in her eyes before glancing away shyly. Or she tends to him after he's hurt with more tenderness than duty demands. Meanwhile, he remembers how she takes her coffee without asking.

Rather than insta-love, incremental awakening conveys authentic yearning. Have one love interest captivated with dawning clarity as she observes her love interest's horse galloping towards home in the distance purely by the rhythm. Or the whiff of her perfume on his shirt startles him awake from dreaming of silky hair slipping through his calloused fingers. Stir all five senses into the attraction cocktail.

Until the reality of risking societal norms or safety protections holding them apart hits. Then, pull back by abruptly separating the leads due to external events or inner turmoil, stoking that longing for lost intimacy, hinting at its irreplaceability. Absence fuels the heart's desire and suspense about whether they will reunite.

Use conflicts mired in historical setting details giving separation credible weight – dangerous prairie weather trapping him far from her homestead for months, family disapproval threatening her inheritance support if she marries beneath station. These reality checks build yearning.

After establishing backstory bonds and initial attraction, chart sexual tension strategically. Tantalizing proximity, like sheltering snugly in an abandoned mine while a snowstorm rages outside, creates temptation. Just one kiss leads to hesitant admission of mutual affection against better judgment. Forbidden pleasures beckon irresistibly.

Now, pull them apart again through renewed external conflict. Vicious cattle ranchers target her homestead for takeover. Threat of violence now endangering new love raises stakes after they briefly tasted bliss. The distance combined with high risk fuels acute longing for reunion, more poignant after knowing affection firsthand. Use this push-pull dynamic to keep readership anxious for eventual romance victory against daunting odds.

Next, gradually build intimacy through gestural confessionals revealing vulnerability seldom shown to anyone else. The first time the gruff cowboy ultimately recounts the boyhood tragedy that left him alone relies on touch as a balm – the brush of her hand on his arm steadies his voice enough to continue. Such quiet moments build bonds through honesty, not grand speeches.

Chart incremental closeness through spatial details too onto ultimate consummation: the toe-curling first kiss giving way to seeking hidden moonlit clearings to exchange fervent caresses without prying eyes, stifled gasps muffled into shoulders, the stolen hours of intimacy in haystacks assaying pleasures of the flesh yet careful not to fully surrender virtue just yet... Finally, conventions fall away fully in the marriage bed for a blissful union.

Through it all, anchor attraction in admiration for character - her courage, his steadfast sense of duty, shared losses suffered, laughter over life's small joys. Build foundations of friendship and understanding before passion's final crescendo. Sustain that substance amidst trials befalling couples destined despite human flaws and mortal frailties. That resilience makes romance victories sweeter.

Strategically stoke sexual/romantic chemistry by establishing emotional bonds before attraction. Then use external conflict to separate lovers, amplifying longing and yearning for reunion. Heart-stirring confessionals build intimacy despite barriers keeping the destined couple apart until; finally, virtue gives way fully to scorching, long-awaited passion!

Supporting Cast

A common pitfall inexperienced writers face is focusing solely on fleshing out Western romance protagonists while neglecting the community surrounding them. Remember, secondary characters offering support, conflict, and wisdom enrich lead character arcs and cement the historical small-town setting your book inhabits.

Populate the landscape with siblings, best friends from childhood, elders passing down generational wisdom and even adversaries who incite external conflict or dispense bitter life lessons. Are stubborn parents dead-set on upholding tradition a barrier for strong-willed ingénues determined to live by their own rules? Do villains play on the fears of supportive confidantes to manipulate isolated protagonists? Build rapport between characters independent of central couples as well through dialogue revealing backstory bonds.

Speaking of parents - fathers primarily demand obedience, enforcing their vision of heirs carrying forth legacies, whether social reputations or family businesses. Mothers, meanwhile, tend to nurture, occasionally defying overbearing patriarchy to defend their children's dreams secretly. However, surprise readers by sometimes reversing tropes. What if the mother insists on tradition while the father sees room for modern roles?

Friends often feature as childhood companionships lasting into adulthood before new romantic relationships test loyalties. The protective, steadfast best friend makes a compelling secondary - especially if unaware of hiding yearning for the lead himself before having to step aside graciously once she finds love with another. This mini-drama tugs heartstrings.

Now take stereotypes but twist them - the native American chef passing down secret family recipes though initially distrusted, the African-American smithy whose extraordinary craft wisely counsels prejudiced townsfolk relying on his services, the female pastor guiding folks spiritually. Diversify perspectives to surprise readership expecting cliched tropes.

For comic relief, the accident-prone ranch foreman, garrulous gossiping seamstress, and other busybodies offer humor through well-meaning interference, complicating the community dynamics and enlivening small frontier towns before everyone inevitably pulls together against common threats.

Atmospheric descriptors using tertiary characters milling about in street markets, school children reciting spelling drills, courtroom observers egging testimony during sensational trials – such vignettes build bustling Old West settings coming alive beyond just the hero and heroine's eye line supporting plot advancement.

Deep poignant backstories for walk-on characters lingering painfully make even brief cameos memorable for readers, Before the grizzled cooked army vet grumbles 'No Charge' accepting food instead of payment for repairing the widow's stove. Little clues hint at bygone youth and idealism.

Have community members impact leads growth arcs through dispensing nuggets of wisdom - the elderly lady gifting the debutante courage with grandmotherly advice or slippery life lessons the cardshark gambler imparts subtly between poker hands before fading back into saloon decor.

Watch out also for trap stereotypes that could perpetuate harmful representation if used thoughtlessly - the drunk, temperamental Irish laborer, for instance. When weaving cultural diversity into characters, seek sensitivity consultation to avoid appropriation. Nuance and substantial roles for everyone remain crucial.

Think also overlapping social circles – your heroine's best friend dating the bartender pursuing your hero's sister, interlinked New World families through multiple generations of offspring. Deep roots spanning years enhance the town's meaning, reminding people to depend on each other and even regulating interference!

Community pressure swaying individual choice tropes manifest intriguingly in romance. Does your steadfast, morally courageous ingénue heroine stand up, refusing the town bigot selected as an eligible husband by matchmaking mothers? Do meddling church ladies nearly sabotage the secret courtship between rival ranching heirs? The power of gossip poses potent threats indeed!

Chapter 7

Developing Plot & Central Conflict

Beyond conveying scenic panoramas or fleshing out rugged solitary cowboy archetypes, the beating heart of any captivating Western romance novel lies in crafting an emotionally resonant central plot and conflict. The narrative traction pushing your lead couple towards confrontation with feelings, life-altering choices, and eventual hard-won resolution stems from how artfully their journey intertwines external events and inner turmoil.

The foundational blueprint guiding story structure should incorporate the hallmarks and conventions of the romance genre that your readership expects while allowing room for fresh innovation. Strategically placed turning points pepper risks of the heart between your rancher searching for purpose after war trauma and a no-nonsense teacher secretly yearning for a steadfast partnership along the road less traveled.

Plenty of templates exist, illustrating the anticipated arc of trials culminating in affirmed commitment. But familiar milestones gain deeper poignancy through personalized context. Does your cowgirl protagonist's fiercely guarded independence stem from childhood emotional neglect and fears of abandoning her struggling family ranch to fate? Do economic machinations by railroad tycoons threatening community displacement echo the buckaroos' inner turmoil?

Beyond romantic arcs, utilize genre flexibility by grafting Western tropes like revenge quests, family feuds, and racial tensions into narratives promising catharsis through hard-fought triumph over corruption. Imaginative plots incorporating historical truths about women's suffrage, immigrant exploitation along the railroad, and pioneering trailblazers make the resonance richer. Secret trysts meet high noon showdowns!

Reference screenwriting guidebook beat sheets if the structure seems intimidating initially. Remember, much flexibility exists between plot points. The key lies in clearly envisioning the protagonist's goals and failed attempts, first raising tension before eventual success wins hearts and minds. Define central conflicts upfront—is it intrapersonal trauma your characters must healthily process to accept love freely offered, or institutional oppression?

Let dramatic action unfurl naturally from characters woven genuinely into the vibrant backdrop a historical Western romance provides. Avenues for engaging plots are abundant, from train heists and abandoned silver mine stake wars to longing glances exchanged at the annual cattle fair. Moving your audience involves keeping protagonists active, shaping stories based on confrontations between moral convictions and realities challenging them at every dusty turn.

When conceptualizing your Western historical romance, understand that readers approach expecting beloved conventions vibrantly delivered through prose conveying adventure and self-discovery rather than just recounting external events. Narrative traction arises from the tension between desire and propriety on the road toward a hard-won happily ever after.

Ensure protagonists are shown seeking love actively from the start, overcoming inner demons and obstacles rather than just reacting to circumstances. Establish a background setting the stage for them recognizing a counterpart able to heal past emotional wounds once walls lower. Build foundations early for characters earning their eventual bombshell first kiss!

Romance arcs differ from generic fiction in that culmination occurs through affirmative commitment between the central couple rather than solitary triumphs alone. Their personal growth feeds off mutual support to overcome external threats. So, position the desire for understanding and belonging as initial motivation rather than base passions alone. Invest readers in their collaborative success.

The narrative core involves romantic tension amplified through raised stakes—will circumstantial secrecy and class differences thwart the ingenue governess and mysterious Byronic stable owner from acting on their smoldering attraction? Utilize misfortune or social forces threatening separation to amplify yearning. A riverside tryst where the cowboy departs at sunrise keeps readers hooked!

Miscommunication tropes are also critical narrative weapons when wielded artfully. Letters gone astray, assumptions bred by jealousy, and prideful refusal to clarify mixed signals all keep mutually pining couples apart! Eventually, confessionals reveal benign reality, strengthening bonds once deception clears. But first, drag out the dramatic irony to agonizing degrees.

As power dynamics shift from initial wariness towards mutual care between couples, have steamier action unfold verbatim without fading to black too early. Specificity and sensuality signal trust earned through partnership on equal footing. But make ultimate sealing encounters hard-won through prolonged yearning stoked through their adventures.

Narrative payoffs build exponentially following the moment destined lovers to relinquish resistance, verbally accepting vulnerability and commitment. Now utilizing terms like 'my beloved' sets readers aflutter since that domestic intimacy bloomed slowly from initial unfamiliarity. High-stakes battles now waged side-by-side pave the way for a ceremonial payoff!

In terms of pacing, locate the romantic declaration, proposal, or passionate kiss as the climax rather than the concluding denouement. Savor an extended resolution showing their new normal settling into committed coupledom while hinting at how their wisdom nurtures community prosperity. Close by conveying a lasting union through symbolism like family heirlooms bequeathed to the next generation.

The alpha cowboy's traditional stoicism and solitary ruggedness alone make for great Westerns, but romance charts lighter revelations. Redemption arrives by accepting he can soften the hardness entrenched since childhood abandonment once the playful ingenue restores his faith in embracing interdependence without shame. She, too, realizes that some vulnerability is nurtured.

Through ups and downs, anchor the narrative in their emotional connection rather than relying solely on external suspense. While obstacles should push couples to breaking points, defined character goals for fulfillment sustain investment building towards affirmations of mutual growth and mainstream bliss.

A common pitfall is portraying the rancher and raven-haired beauty's chemistry through physical attributes alone, risking superficiality. Revealing intellectual rapport through spirited repartee and philosophical musing makes an emotional coup de foudre convincing when initial peril throws them together grudgingly before affection sparks.

Inciting Incident and Call to
Adventure

Western romance novels immediately grab the reader's attention by quickly establishing a disruptive inciting incident that throws ordered worlds into chaos right on the opening pages before the dust even settles. Avoid genteel intros better suited for drawing-room comedies of errors! Kick off with excitement instead!

Classic examples might include a high-stakes robbery gone wrong on a show train headed to a frontier boomtown, a wayward shot in the middle of skirmishes between posse men and native tribal warriors, or an ominous clash with grizzly bears upending a young lady's nature sketching expedition, resulting in a rugged stranger risking life and limb to guarantee her safety.

The inciting incident in a Western romance is not just about throwing the protagonist into chaos. It's also about foreshadowing the core conflict brewing beneath the surface. This could be a conflict between individuals or mighty institutions. By hinting at these gathering storms, the inciting incident creates suspense and anticipation, keeping the reader hooked.

Challenge stereotypes by portraying heroines as resilient and proactive in times of crisis. Instead of helpless females in need of rescue, depict them as the first to respond, attempting to mediate conflicts or defuse tense situations. This shift in narrative will empower your audience and inspire them to see beyond traditional gender roles.

This dramatic opening incident implies the 'call to adventure' archetypal milestone, signaling leads dragged out of complacency into strange, unpredictable territory. External threats trigger personal epiphanies—the wayward debutante fleeing etiquette suddenly responsible for orphaned charges when their caretaker falls critically ill during the journey west, or militiamen ambushed en route to joining regiments out East now squaring off against former comrades turned mercenary marauders.

When the inciting events thrust your protagonists into unfamiliar and challenging situations, ensure that the emotional beats resonate with your audience. Connect these emotional moments to the characters' desires or fears, amplifying them through the conflict. This will deepen the audience's connection with the characters and keep them emotionally invested in the story.

Rather than fixating completely on dangers posed by Western landscapes unique to pioneer settlers, explore social threats as well—church deacon hypocrisy, the devastating reputation of innocents caught in gossip crossfire with no opportunity to clear their names, or railroad stock speculation robbing common folk of entire family savings without recompense. Forces beyond simple East vs. West existence prove compelling, too.

Overall, sharply convey chaos inflicted suddenly through that inciting gunshot, stampede, train robbery, or whatever urgent plot device you deploy, instantly threatening emotional equilibrium just as characters find tentative stability in worlds already filled with tumultuous uncertainty given the historical upheaval of frontier life! Shake foundations. Then whisk them away onto unfamiliar trails where the worst and best await!

Sources of Conflict

For Western romance protagonists, navigating the harsh realities of frontier life often clashes with their deep desire for true love. Traditional family values and customs exert a strong influence. Parents may insist on prearranged, financially secure matches, disregarding their children's hearts. Inheritance might hinge on marrying someone from an acceptable social class, making defiance a risky gamble with security.

Bitter family feuds, simmering for generations over water rights, grazing land, or other vital resources, can further complicate love stories. Oral histories keep these grievances alive, fueling deep mistrust between families. Finding peace can demand significant sacrifices.

The rugged frontier lifestyle itself presents a constant danger. Range riders face peril every day, from wrangling, bucking broncos, and managing cattle drive through treacherous terrain to battling predators and unpredictable weather. Even without the threat of outlaws, which was relatively rare in sparsely populated areas, the work itself is a constant threat to life and limb.

For independent-minded leading ladies, defying societal expectations comes with its own set of challenges. Formal education is limited, and employment opportunities are largely confined to domestic spheres. Financial dependence on male relatives creates pressure to marry "well" and young. Those who don't conform risk gossip, sanctions from the church or family, or even complete shunning. Unmarried women without support networks face a social death sentence.

Early courtship throws additional hurdles. Rivals vying for affection may emerge – a former flame returning or a mysterious stranger captivating the town. Whispers of the heroine's past indiscretions can spark jealousy in her beau. Who will be the first to confront the rumors?

Geographic isolation breeds suspicion towards newcomers. In these close-knit communities, unfamiliar faces can disrupt the status quo. Perhaps a land grab fueled by speculation threatens local ownership, or a wealthy heiress attracts fortune hunters.

For those seeking prosperity, divisions between settlers and indigenous tribes can be exploited. Corrupt officials fan the flames of hostility to justify land grabs. Tribal youth witnessing the erosion of their traditions by encroaching homesteaders and industrial interests add a layer of social commentary relevant even today.

Threats go beyond the stereotypical outlaw. Cattle barons may use questionable methods to expand their empires. Crooked railway agents divert vital supplies, while gambling hall owners exploit locals through deception. Even seemingly legitimate figures – shady doctors with lax ethics – can pose a significant danger.

Instead of constant action sequences, delve into the intricate social dynamics. Focus on the gossiping aunts who meddle in matchmaking, the judgmental deacons, and the awkward attempts at reconciliation between distrustful Native American tribes and white settlements. These interpersonal tensions often hold the key to character development and self-reflection.

Ultimately, the yearning for authentic connection lies at the heart of these stories. Protagonists long for someone who "sees" them beyond the masks they wear for society. Secret courtships reveal their true selves – the gambler running a den of chance or the exiled debutante working as a lowly tutor. Let their essential humanity shine through.

Raising Stakes and Obstacles
to Love

The harsh beauty of the untamed West sets a dramatic backdrop for burgeoning romance. Nature's unpredictable fury mirrors the inner turmoil of protagonists who must lower their emotional guard, risking vulnerability. External threats constantly test the bonds between these distrustful souls as they slowly recognize kindred spirits yearning for genuine connection.

The gruff ranch foreman bristles at the arrival of the new headmistress. She disrupts his routine, advocating "civilizing" the ranch hands with Eastern education. Yet, her gentle empathy chips away at the walls he's built since his soldier days. Her delicate health, a stark contrast to his rugged exterior, hints at a hidden past. Meanwhile, their stolen glances suggest deeper regrets and a yearning for a connection missed.

Shared hardships forge reluctant bonds. Facing external threats, these protagonists find excuses for closeness, allowing them to momentarily forget the walls separating their worlds. But propriety's constraints loom large. Can these disparate backgrounds truly intertwine beyond fleeting moments, or will societal obligations tear them apart, forcing them into difficult choices?

Obstacles arise, testing the bridges they've cautiously built. Parental pressure pushes "wayward" offspring to abandon dreams of independence. Bank foreclosures threaten homesteaders, while whispers of past relationships ignite jealousy despite attempts to move on.

Situational conflicts also complicate their journeys. Work-site injuries force recovery under one another's roofs, straining virtue as desire simmers. Underhanded sabotage by competitors throws them together, while harsh weather forces shared campouts, blurring the lines of propriety to ensure survival.

For protagonists grappling with past trauma, vulnerability poses a risk. Revealing intimate confessions, especially those stemming from the Civil War, might trigger rejection. Emotional scars run deep, making hearts guarded.

Fate also throws its curveballs. Childbirth complications, terminal illness, or sudden deaths force agonizing choices: duty versus love. Such blows test their resolve, threatening the optimism that propelled them towards hope and prosperity on the frontier.

Societal constraints add another layer of complexity. Religious objections, racial prejudices, and class differences can all disrupt potential unions. Social standing plays a crucial role in determining romantic outcomes.

Defiance, particularly for women, comes with a price. Unmarried women are vulnerable and ostracized as "spinsters" by harsh townsfolk. Rumors can quickly spread, jeopardizing the reputation of a kind and gentle schoolmarm despite her dedication to her students.

Financial woes constantly thwart the hero's ability to provide for a future family. Bad investments, unscrupulous bankers, poor harvests, and livestock disease – all historical realities that could shatter dreams of homesteading and respectable marriage.

Natural disasters exacerbate existing tensions. Cattle plagues, devastating wildfires, and brutal winters can decimate resources and test the resilience of relationships.

In conclusion, the untamed frontier presents a myriad of challenges for budding romances. By weaving historical details with creativity, you can craft compelling narratives where love triumphs over societal boundaries and external threats. The final union of these "destined darlings" will be all the more satisfying for having endured such adversity.

Tying it all together

Building toward an emotionally resonant climax and delivering cathartic release becomes paramount once romantic protagonists overcome a series of escalating obstacles keeping them apart temporarily. Have faith your readers feel sufficiently invested in the lead characters' fates by this juncture, having endured those escalating roller-coaster tensions throughout the rising action. They expect supremely hard-won and meaningful resolutions earned authentically!

Revisit core desires propelling protagonists since page one to remind why their personal yearnings justified struggles witnessed previously. Was the feisty saloon proprietress merely seeking prosperity on her terms, eschewing suffocating patriarchal expectations of womanhood back east? Did wanderlust possess the cowpoke rambler initially until a meaningful connection grounded his roving heart? Whatever core desires mattered most, remind the audience through nostalgic callbacks as part of tying finales together neatly.

Look also for what external symbolic milestones these travelers, starting from wildly divergent points, have achieved that now unite them around shared values worth preserving. Homeland acreage ownership finally secured against bandits constantly threatening violence, for example, reflects peace attained domestically. Personal growth accepting vulnerability strengthens rather than weakens their fiber. Let the landscapes echo the characters' centeredness reached over time!

While the relationship itself occupies the centerpiece in resolutions, don't forget enriching layers regarding larger community lives interconnected in tight-knit frontier settlements where individuals' repercussions have far-reaching consequences. Did this marriage solve deep-rooted social strife, too, through its example of former foes coming together into one family bloodline poised to heal generational wounds? Significance amplifies satisfaction levels!

Characters' arc completions also matter, highlighting how journeys altered values and personalities through enlightenment reached over the pages. Now, the snooty aristocrat might cast aside haughty snobbery, recognizing the common democratic dreams that unite all classes struggling together. Prejudice dissolves through humbling experiences, having worn down those former barriers dividing folk. Thematic resonance remains critical besides just reconnecting lovers somehow.

On more private, intimate notes, objects carrying symbolic importance carry extra narrative heft. Ancestral wedding rings or pocket watches imbue sentimental payoff, expounding on founded futures and building new collective legacies in chapters chronicling their story. Do specific wardrobe items discarded, like boots or native beadwork adopted, signal metamorphosing transformations embracing unexpected destinies? Select deliberate visual cues mirroring denouement meanings!

Locations carry powerful associative memories for readers, too, based on their significance to the story. Imagine vows exchanged at the same secluded grassy meadows where passions first ignited in secret; ancestral homesteads cleared through great toil becoming appropriate shelters for ceremony commemorations; desert canyons where outlaws repented, offering isolation permitting confessional dialogue bonding love interests beforehand.

Natural imagery also provides poignant apertures into plot resolution writing itself. Ending chapters amidst the first gentle rains blessing parched croplands after a devastating drought perfectly captures renewed hope and the cyclical return of abundance following hardship. Pregnant silences acknowledging storms weathered sketch contented smiles of proud survivors vanquishing uncertainty – all powerful notes upon drawing the curtains closed!

Even incidental movement conveys levels of newfound unification despite differences finally put aside. Look for moments where the contrasting stances of the partners are visually shown by them standing hand-in-hand peering towards horizons no longer daunting. Gradually coming together as problems dissolve, the distancing between them reinforces the spiritual merge sealed thematically.

Finales require final considerations beyond ceremonial kisses or buzzword phrases like "happily ever after" tacked on willy-nilly. Which loose ends need addressing? Orphaned children rescued from outlaws being adopted officially? Retired outlaws themselves finding ranch-hand employment? Laws were enacted, establishing newly founded towns with churches and jails simultaneously. Audiences expect holistic completeness, reaffirming order in ways that pay off the intensive arcs.

Inevitably, climactic romance peaks involve lusty intimacy liberated from restraint at long last as lovers, torn asunder, come together as one spiritually and physically against all odds! But craft these intense moments carefully, walking a sweet tightrope between metaphorical purple prose, vulgarities, and cliched vagueness lacking punch. Subtle innuendo suggesting movement conveys everything while leaving richer details deliciously for readers' imaginations to run wild!

Chapter 8

Writing Sex Scenes

Amid sweeping frontier vistas and high-stake gunslinger showdowns, some of Western romance's most pivotal narrative moments occur when friction between star-crossed lovers finally combusts into smoldering physical passion. While the genre skews towards inspirational love conquering all, readers devour deliciously rendered intimate encounters elevating bodice-ripping clichés into something far more scorching.

From Claire Marti's " The Outlaw's Redemption" blazing opening of a former criminal cynically seducing the town's sweet new schoolmarm for ulterior motives to Leigh Greenwood's " Powerful Pendragon" culminating scene finally consummating years of denied yearning between bitter rivals reluctantly co-running a cattle empire, examples abound where choreographed ardor between sheets sparks imaginations aflame.

However, authors must deftly walk tightropes between conveying enough sensual frankness satisfying audiences while avoiding off-putting levels of gratuitousness potentially alienating other demographics drawn to western flavor beyond just erotic indulgences. Consider guidelines from target publishers as industry preferences vary across inspirational versus steamy romance gradings.

Bestselling authors find workarounds presenting impressionistic innuendo rather than clinical explicitness by weaving symbolism into character interactions focusing on emotional resonance trumping crude anatomy breakdowns - Charlie Craven's " Hell to Pay" notably capturing bristling chemistry when scruffy antihero Ben clashes reuniting with ex-lover Grace after prison stint through potent metaphors like "raking his gaze ravenously from her tousled hair down to boots splayed brazenly open."

Much evocative power stems from emphasis on primal emotions reveled in stolen moments finally consummating forbidden desires long skirting proprieties of the era rather than strictly explicit body part spreadsheets - Johanna Lindsey's modern classic " Warrior's Woman" illustrates heat building believable rising tensions between army scout Jared and feisty stranger Liza surviving tortuous ordeals together before even one kiss lands.

Movement proves key portraying vigor exchanged powerfully sans excessive coarseness - " Elizabeth Lowell's Only

You" describes unbridled motion through symbolic verbiage "like wild horses galloping uninhibited across open grasslands" rather than fixating solely on raunchy specifics of tussled sheets as headboards knock. Innuendoes appeal further imagining more vividly than gynecological clinical textbook recitations allow.

Consider context environments respectfully associated with tastes - a hastily pitched bedroll outside wagon encampment connotes impromptu intimacy crackling urgently, whereas pausing lengthy bedroom seduction journeys allows opportunity savoring slower buildup through layers of undressing. Westerns provide locale variety amplifying atmospheric sensuality accordingly.

Escalate rising action through artful restraint and patience - part the appeal lies in torturous accumulation of pent-up lust shouldn't felt immediately assuaged between would-be lovebirds separated by plots' meddling barring gratifications yet. Frame consummation fulfilling arcs capping journeys rather than random hookups drained of excitement. Diana Palmer's " Wyoming Fierce" artistically captures such enduring through discrete fades-to-black still gratifying after Gib finally admits Mallory matters.

Most importantly, credible Western romance encounters epitomize authentic characterizations developed over lengthy investment - an educated chaste debutante only recently located virtue tested overnight by entirely new frontiers' awakening primal instincts; a coolly cynical bounty hunter letting accidentally witnessing target's intimate vulnerabilities unexpectedly stir long-dormant compassions etc. Relate interpersonal emotional continuities elevating significance beyond meaningless hedonism.

Use sex scenes highlighting turning points exposing inner selves stripped bare - Rosanne Bittner's epics like " Nightbird" memorably turn the bedroom into transformative existential conduits altering self-perceptions where long-held judgments dissolve facing true souls loving every single scar behind closed doors. Readers should feel raptures beyond orgasms alone feeling power dynamics recalibrated permanently!

When it comes to crafting steamy, yet tasteful love scenes set on the frontier, word choice proves critical differentiating prose celebrating intimacy's delicate beauty from shallow smut letters. Powerful sensory details trumping gratuitous vulgarity forge unforgettable literary romps leaving readers breathlessly flushed.

Avoid robotic clinicalisms favoring flowery creativity - rather than "he inserted his engorged member" try Rosanne

Bittner's lush metaphor from "Thunder on the Plains" : "he sheathed himself in her softness, their joining as natural as rain quenching parched earth." See how lyricism enhances romance through naturalistic verses mechanical pornography?

Look to classic love poetry inspirations for subtle evocative vocabulary enriching Western amours without explicit profanities - Terri Osburn summons Shakespeare's famous "my mistress' eyes are nothing like the sun" underpinnings updating "Sun-bronzed skin aglow from honest toil, wayward curls framing eyes outshining Montana's Big Sky." Unleash your inner bard!

Frontier landscapes infuse symbolism into modern Western icons transcending anatomical tedium - build anticipation honing familiar genre touchstones sensually repurposed like Katherine Sutcliffe's "Wrangler's Reform" passage "pent-up longing ready to buck tempestuously as mustang meeting his first filly of spring."

However, indulging lyrical fancy shouldn't eclipse relatability prioritizing obscure metaphors distancing readers from protagonists' emotional truth - Linda Howard grounds "Midnight Rainbow" bedroom romps respecting cowboy authenticity with earthy exchanges like "Damn darlin'...hold on tight as you can." Vernacular enhances atmospheric veracity.

Still, proceed judiciously balancing verisimilitude against archaisms lapsing into unintentional camp territory - "L'Amour's Bendigo Shafter" straddles cleverly "Her slender tan fingers traced valleys and prairies of muscle" versus unintentionally silly" cage poised to unlock and release his mighty eagle." Moderation separates serious literature from self-parody.

* * *

Masterfully scripting Western romance love scenes involves far more than tossing protagonists between tangled sheets spouting lusty dialogue meant solely titillating readers physically. Emotional authenticity and narrative purpose must underscore steamy prose or risk "wedge in" pornography missing bigger picture intimacy. So what separates shallow sensationalism from moving high art celebrating bonds transcending carnality?

Several structural layers constitute seductive literary prowess subtly choreographing interludes spotlighting more than coitus mechanics. Atmospheric buildup sets stages conveying longing through spatial relationships gradually closing from initial wary awareness towards magnetic attraction overpowering restraint – consider Diana Palmer's tortured Tycoon Cord slowly realizing loyal ranch manager Maris arouses unfamiliar feelings despite professional boundaries once casual touches linger longer than appropriate at the *Rancho Real*.

Flirtatious innuendo through sparse but weighted romantic banter also stokes appetites before contact. Sharp repartee reveals inner traits attractive contrasting external façades further humanizing characters. Even as locked gazes convey wordless confessions, have past pains and secrets surface too deepening complexity behind simplistic trysts. Readers invest witnessing pivotal self-discoveries unfolding through sexual catharsis.

Once impatient passions spill over polite niceties into impulsive urges, describe mounting sensations employing all five senses besides obligatory visual cues - *Elizabeth Lowell's Only His* transports with sultry adjectives "rain-water yielding to scorching desire, the sweet heady smell of want mingling with sagebrush" utilizing frontier ambiance furthering seduction's impact. Dusty cotton shifts become impatient obstacles rather than just dull laundry.

While concise interludes prove effective when prior chapters piled deliberately exhausting "will they, won't they?" slow-burn tension, earning climactic releases demands acknowledging physical and emotional continuities. Show afterglow Dom moments bonding intimacy stronger than surface lust. Have Jo Goodman's hesitant shopkeep swallowing prideful uncertainty before confessing long-buried traumas to Reed post-coitus. Exposed vulnerability follows ecstasy.

Now faded lights promise new beginnings with dawn - escalate conflicts even amid domestic bliss given external threats remain. Perhaps gossiping biddies naysay legitimacy; disapproving parents sever financial backing, former beaus resurface nurturing jealous doubts etc. Hard-earned happiness remains precarious on dangerous frontier fringes always encroaching. Sustain dramatic urgency keeping readership hooked invested in heroic outcomes.

Overall remember eroticism effective when furthering character growth and cementing romantic arcs organically, not spliced gratuitously likeSir Walter Scott awkwardly transitioning Ivanhoe plot into sudden graphic orgies tangential abandoning previous action. Each sensual detail should reveal motivations and personality dimensions deepening attraction's poignancy.

Describe environments' symbolism enhancing or possibly inhibiting vulnerability levels between would-be sweethearts like Charlie Craven's *The Bitterroot Inn's* hard-drinking cardshark finding public piano performances by the mysterious songbird strangely more intimate and disarming than performative seductions with countless paramours beforehand. Context adds meaning.

While male scarred antiheroes escaping tortured pasts through the affections of nurturing heroines proves popular archetype even today, flip assumptions letting historically stoic cowgirls initiate intimacy plainly on personal terms upending traditional power dynamics — as Jo Goodman's blacksmith heroine in *Only Herself* unabashedly leads with "Best finish undressing afore you make me lose patience, Xavier O'Conner." Celebrate feminine sexual agency embracing desires.

Eschew gender assumptions dictating carnal modalities - fold playful elements like Lorelei James' *Unbridled* scene with tomboy Ace coyly deploying naughty silk ropes and candy treats into loveplay adding spice while obeying unique partner personalities beyond cookie cutter domination/submission stereotypes needlessly gendered. Character authenticity intrigues.

While fade-to-black ellipses prove necessary acknowledging audience age diversity beyond just passionate consenting adults, utilize discretion without abruptly abandoning tangible sensuality ratcheting arousals peaking. Poignant parting visuals etched into imaginations substitutes lacking explicit follow-through - burning lantern flames extinguished hint plenty.

Western literary tryst artistry involves masterfully elevating intercourse connecting souls beyond mechanics servicing transient lust by spotlighting vulnerability, humor, playfulness revealing protagonists stripped off all emotional armor. Bypassing gratuitous anatomy drooling for multifaceted takeaways making brief encounters resonate through entire relationship arcs transforms meaningless copulation into profound erogenous genius!

While passion sparks fly portraying romantic leads' irresistible magnetism, transform intimate encounters into pivotal milestones advancing overall story arcs. Use scorching tension spilling over thresholds as launch pads highlighting progression from earlier inhibitions into liberating self-discovery through uninhibited intimacy gradually emboldening protagonists in defiance against daunting external threats still seeking destroying hard-won happiness.

Potent intrapersonal epiphanies emerge amid breathless throes entangled conveying empowerment - initially skittish Sarah finally baring hidden scars permitting vulnerability after Sam's patient affections coax confessionals assuaging survivor's guilt haunting commentary avoidance before. Such cumulations feel cathartic, not contrived detours stalling narratives if properly laid groundwork beforehand established character motivations making physical trysts pay narrative dividends beyond just displaying bodies intertwined purely readers superficial enjoyment.

Outlaw JJ teaching runaway bride, Celia alien terrains surrendering without losing independence as they chart constellations overhead, "Naked halfway beneath endless night skies making earthly barriers feel wonderfully insignificant beheld up close firsthand". Such metaphoric moments emphasize liberation's double meaning - embracing desires fully while fearlessly chasing autonomous destinies. Make descriptive details resonate symbolically this way.

Reputational consequences raise stakes post intimacy against unforgiving backdrops - has societal pedestal for ranch magnate Wayne's pristine heir reputation irrevocably cracked *after fleeting indiscretion inside the barn with his son's rambunctious rodeo rival Jenny*; thereby spawning a chaotic sequence of reactions from mortified kith, kin and judgmental frontier church deacons? Let private actions precipitate public storms!

Plot-wise utilize 'morning-after' scenarios as post-coitus crucibles revealing true emotional depths between partners - does masculine shame make Dalton flee April's cottage unable handling affection shown behind closed doors...or does newfound tenderness make this gruff saddlebum linger awhile gently tracing the sleeping seamstress' cheekbone appreciating her peaceful beauty at sunrise after guarding away all protective pretense stripped bare night before? Nuances fascinate!

Fade-to-black scenes tactfully acknowledging intimacy consummated later remain useful devices too, so long as symbolism conveys significance through crisp impactful parting visuals etched vividly into reader minds. Lantern flames extinguished; darkness enshrouds silhouettes seamlessly morphing into one. Powerful punctuation without raunchy play-by-plays.

However, eschewing graphic sensationalism risks romanticizing carnality without substance leaving shallow tropes. Ensure descriptive passages before fireworks convey why such intensity shared by *these specific people* makes tearful sense based established investments appreciating pains suffered and dues paid beforehand now finding cathartic absolutions and safe harbor within fiduciary arms finally lowering barricades after lifetimes steeling solitary defenses against further emotional eviscerations feared since youth but miraculously scars reopening now heals gently unless themes established first about redemptive qualities found from intimacy itself.

Emphasize uniqueness between protagonists making them irresistible only toward each other despite surround options more socially suitable by frontier standards. Contextualize their combo against community norms and past relationships trying capturing lightning in a bottle this second time around ending violation cycles once destructive but flipped through uplifting reciprocation repairing damage inflicted by previous exes. The ' 'manic pixie dream girl' trope symbolic of characters catalyst convenience enabling leads alone progressing without dimensionality themselves should be avoided however in modern inclusion cautions removing token objectifications.

Still infusion responsibility beyond carnal satiations lingers long afterwards charging environments with portentous energies mirrored by characters undergoing marked evolutions through boudoir breakthroughs reaching clarity from pleasure-induced deliriums alone initially sought self-serving "but unexpectedly awakened latent honesty admitting reciprocal affections through tearful laughter easing lifelong burdens shared finally with willing safe harbor partners lifting equal weights deserving renowned through oral cowboy historical folk ballads retold for posterity despite debaucherous undertones morally ambiguous on surfaces but profound in poesy."

Sensual language conveys multiple connotations that experienced authors amplify cleverly. A buckle eventually opened hinting promise. Dark stares conveyed wordless confessionals. Such subtle literary devices require far richer imaginative engagements from participants savored longer than overtly spelling raunchy vocabulary overly graphic erasing mystery conjured organically through innuendo and atmospheric scene settings alone allowing readers unique personal interpretations filling gaps based on tastes without forcibly subjecting all equally towards gratuitous passages better left private not flashed vainly like trophy accomplishments but sacred gesture between committed protagonists no further exploiting clinical anatomies now poetically entwined.

Chapter 9

Getting the Details Right

When transporting readers into bygone eras, prioritize meticulous research to vividly resurrect authentic details that breathe life into your story. Factual accuracy lends credibility and immerses audiences in long-lost worlds, allowing them to trust your narrative enough to get swept away by the romantic journey.

Seemingly minor elements like characters' everyday garments, tools, vocabularies, and social etiquette norms can make or break suspension of disbelief if rendered convincingly. In "Francine Rivers' acclaimed Redeeming Love," Angel's 1850s California wardrobe of crinoline petticoats beneath swishing silk skirts immediately establishes the Gold Rush atmosphere and her precarious existence as a saloon girl yearning for better horizons.

To master such period minutiae, frequent museums showcasing Old West ephemera like the Autry Museum of the American West in Los Angeles or the Buffalo Bill Center of the West in Cody, Wyoming. Examine antique homestead furniture, prairie schooner wagons, blacksmithing equipment, rifles, and textiles up close while imagining how your characters would interact with these artifacts daily.

Historical societies and preservation organizations also offer invaluable resources through archived journals, letters, and photographs documenting frontier lifestyles and mindsets. Read pioneer memoirs and 19th-century newspapers to absorb dialect cadences and attitudes for different regions, eras, and social classes. Jot down colorful slang and idiomatic turns of phrase to sprinkle into dialogue later.

When describing settings, reference vintage maps surveying township layouts, railroads, and geographic landmarks that shaped community development. "Beverly Jenkins" excels at recreating African American havens like 1870s Kansas in "Tempest" where horse breeder Regan's all-Black town of Paradise thrives as an agricultural jewel amidst nearby Confederate prejudice, based on Jenkins' extensive research into real Black settlements.

Fashion history remains crucial for precisely dressing characters according to their time, socioeconomic status, and occupation. A rebellious rancher's daughter in dungarees will scandalously defy expectations compared to a demure banker's daughter in ruffled silk. Paging through digitized pattern catalogs from the era can suggest fabrics, cuts, and trims for key outfits, turning looks into statements.

When outfitting cowboys and lawmen, get weapon terminology accurate to showcase expertise that seasoned shooters will appreciate. Familiarize yourself with the differences between Colt Single Action Army revolvers, Winchester repeating rifles and derringers to arm heroes appropriately for their skill level and profession. Peruse gun collectors' encyclopedias to avoid embarrassing anachronisms.

Culinary history provides another avenue for sumptuous sensory details anchoring scenes in delectable specificity. "Tina Radcliffe's Claiming Her Cowboy" evokes 1880s Nebraska through boarding house owner Lucy's hardtack biscuits and green tomato pickle recipes reflecting frontier staples and seasonal preservation techniques. Your foodie readers will savor the extra effort at mouthwatering meals.

Indigenous representation warrants sensitive consultation with tribe members to ensure customs, beliefs, and languages are portrayed respectfully without stereotypes. "Rosanne Bittner's Mystic Dreamers series" deeply immerses in 1830s Lakota culture by working closely with descendants sharing oral histories and traditions, honoring their resilience and romance amidst White encroachment threatening cherished lifestyles.

However, beware of info-dumping exhaustive minutiae at the expense of character development and momentum. Dribble fun facts naturally through action and conversation rather than halting scenes for dry lectures. "Jo Goodman's" deft incorporation of 1870s San Francisco Barbary Coast details through "Never Love a Lawman's" Wyatt and Rachel's witty flirtatious banter exemplifies organic exposition that educates and entertains.

Instead of frontloading novels with excessive historical context, reveal background incrementally as it impacts characters' everyday lives, major decisions, and romantic complications. Gradually paint political and socioeconomic landscapes through overheard gossip at the general store, editorials in local broadsheets, and sermons at Sunday church socials where peer pressure reinforces behavioral expectations.

When imagining characters' inner lives, extrapolate judiciously from modern psychology while still respecting historical realities that would shape worldviews. A 19th-century debutante heroine can plausibly wrestle with timeless fears of spinsterhood and desire for independence, but her options for pursuing non-marital fulfillment will be

far more limited compared to her contemporary coun-
terparts.

Ground courtship rituals and flirtations in era-appropriate
gender norms dictating proper conduct between the sexes.
Research prevailing religious doctrines, age of consent
statutes, and marital property laws to determine how much
alone time your couples can realistically steal without
causing irreparable scandal. "Francine Rivers' The Atone-
ment Child" thoughtfully depicts 1890s premarital sex's
devastating ostracism for the heroine.

Avoid projecting overly modern sensibilities onto historical
characters navigating constricted social mobility and
entrenched prejudices with far fewer legal protections
than we enjoy today. Even if you intend a tale of empowerment, your spunky heroines can't singlehandedly overturn
systemic inequities overnight without pushback. "Beverly
Jenkins" strikes this balance deftly in "Tempest's" post-
bellum interracial romance.

At the same time, don't feel compelled to regurgitate textbook timelines at the expense of emotional truth. If you
unearth a fascinating footnote that ignites your imagination, indulge that spark of invention! "Courtney Milan's"
marvelously unconventional heroines pursuing
unorthodox livelihoods like paleontology in "The Dinosaur
Hunter's Daughter" encourage us to dream bigger within
any era's strictures.

So meticulously chosen props, fashions, foods, and vocabulary resurrect gritty Old West atmosphere while still serving a larger story purpose. Sprinkle salient details like trail dust baked into straw hat brims and burnished gun grips to paint cinematic visuals. But ultimately, breathe life into history through vividly realized inner landscapes reflecting each generation's aspirations, hypocrisies and hard-won triumphs.

By marrying exhaustive book learning with bold leaps of imagination, historical Western romances can unearth poignant parallels between distant past and contemporary struggles. Whether a plucky heroine is escaping a tyrannical father's arranged marriage plot or a haunted hero is resisting his reform school sweetheart's temptation to fall back into outlaw ways, their timeless fears and forbidden yearnings still resonate across centuries.

So don't feel pigeonholed by 19th-century frontier clichés confining Native Americans to wise shaman sidekicks and Mexican vaqueros to exotic sultry troublemakers. "Rosanne Bittner's" success reimagining Westward Expansion from indigenous first-person perspectives in "Mystic Dreamers" proves readers crave complex multi-ethnic narratives restoring erased histories through the eternal power of love.

Therefore, when writing historical Western romances, celebrate the iconic Stetsons and spurs, stagecoaches, and stockyards that first stoked your own nostalgic passion for a bygone Americana. But open your heart even wider to the uncharted territories of marginalized lives still awaiting swoon-worthy happily-ever-afters that only your singularly fearless voice can finally manifest on the page!

Chapter 10

Sound Authentic

When writing dialogue, you must strike a delicate balance by invoking iconic cowboy vernacular without lapsing into corny caricature. Study speech cadences from the late 1800s frontier era to absorb quaint rural diction accurately while still sounding natural. Then, judiciously sprinkle in select cowboy lingo to enhance local flavor.

Consider the rhythms in dialogue like "Cord glared at her, jaw tight. 'Reckon you'd best go help out in the kitchen, little lady,'" which establishes gruff but gentlemanly courtship staples meeting fierce feminine defiance. Compare speech patterns by region and class too - East Coast aristocracy enunciated more precisely following elocution training compared to casual frontier settlers speaking with relaxed grammar. Nevada prospectors and Oregon trailblazers adopted words from French Canadian trappers or Spanish vaqueros, reflecting migration influences.

Cowboy lexicon terms resonate charmingly when used judiciously by characters who would realistically know that specialized terminology from lived experience - farriers, rodeo riders, and livestock herders. But avoid awkward overkill that feels gimmicky, detracting from the story flow. Study the etymology behind quaint terms before placing them seamlessly into the appropriate context.

However, some outdated terms require due diligence, checking etymological baggage - injudicious words risk unintentionally alienating modern diverse readership through racial microaggressions or sexism. Rather than excusing offensive slurs as "true to the times," consider thoughtful substitutions conveying identical moods while prioritizing inclusive accessibility without compromising atmospheric authenticity.

Speech mannerisms signaling background and temperament bring characters alive vividly on the page beyond just vocabulary itself. Stoic types prone to silence reveal personalities through a few gruff words weighted with meaning, while effusive chatterboxes provide clues through their stream-of-consciousness nattering. Knowing character experiences through backstories determines outward communication modes flavored by upbringing.

Beyond crafting distinct dialogue exchanges per persona, avoid interaction dynamics growing stale and predictable. Surprise readers by swapping roles - the laconic cowboy suddenly gushing effusively or the perky ingénue sharply retorting skepticism. Inject vulnerability, contempt, enthusiasm, etc., spontaneously to keep exchanges intriguing.

Study Emmy-nominated shows like "Deadwood" and contemporary Westerns ("Longmire," "Cowboy Bebop") for adapting slang into accessible screenwriting without anachronisms or affectations. Note speech mannerisms signaling roots and temperaments through rural versus urban vernaculars, class consciousness, and gender roles. Then adapt those cinematic storytelling tools for compelling book dialogue that sounds comfortably authentic coming from rustic Western characters or futuristic frontiers.

Keep exposition conversational rather than preachy monologues. Reveal attitudes and backstories subtly through throwaway gossip between minor characters rather than inserting obvious chunks of oral tradition mythmaking that flags readers about cowboy creation lore being shared next. Scatter meaningful flavor dialogue tags setting scenes too - words acknowledging gestures small but symbolically resonant like "He held his hat respectfully as the funeral procession passed" or "She jutted out her chin defiantly." Such parsings establish unspoken dynamics and power balances, energizing moods wordlessly through body language and actions.

Ultimately, the delicate goal is to balance achieving atmospheric historical sprinkles without weirdly anachronistic diction that disrupt sentences, catching the reader's attention negatively. A light hand with liberal cowboy colloquialisms blended into the textural backdrop keeps interest without heavy focal points, making attempts clunkily obvious. Rhythms matter more than perfect grammar in fictional frontier folks' speech meant to represent diverse communities shaped through oral histories like exaggerated tall tales!

Overall, meticulously listen to how actual speech shapes realities by flavoring phrases reflecting upbringing, geographic isolation, and social values beyond just vocabulary alone. Note unspoken volumes revealed from silence, lies, bemusement, and outrage manifesting through distinct vernaculars. Then, recreate expository dialogue organically through marginalized viewpoints overlooked in mythic cowboy frontiers, sharing universal stories of love persevering against oppression that today's audiences crave hearing, awarded attention previously denied historically.

Chapter 11

Here Comes the Hard Part - Marketing

Beyond typing "The End," a new arduous yet exhilarating phase lies ahead that you must master to survive in the publishing game: marketing your work through savvy positioning to ensure readers discover and become devoted fans of the cowboy romance genre you brought to life through blood, sweat, and deletion keystrokes. Do niche research first to identify potential superfans before deploying irresistible campaigns to recruit future loyal brand ambassadors.

Know the core Western romance readership well through both market research data and engaging directly in niche online communities across romance review blogs and forums, Facebook groups celebrating beloved tropes, and Twitter hashtag discussions ranking favorite cowboy book boyfriends. Follow fan accounts enthusiastically, highlighting beloved series staples, and study what resonates through loving memes and commentary.

Once patterns emerge around favorite character archetypes, settings, plot devices, and emotional payoffs, conceptualize your book's unique positioning by blending recognizable genre expectations, yet compelling readers with a fresh perspective never spotlighted before in previous frontier romance tales. Analyze recent bestselling debuts to distinguish the new voices that led to success.

For instance, notice that many Old West stories are framed through white, cisgender, heteronormative, patriarchal perspectives. So perhaps you can diversify by centering authentically nuanced indigenous experiences or explore a "transgender settler's journey" participating in pioneering westward migration reflecting shifting frontiers both geographical and social. The wide-open prairie symbolizes boundless possibilities for reinventing Western romance!

Concise logline pitches distilling stories into irresistible high-concept taglines will appeal immensely to time-strapped fans inundated with infinite reading choices. Study analogous television show premises boiled down into single sentences that capture the essence quickly, then convey your story similarly through a provocative book logline, reducing the manuscript sprawl into tantalizing soundbites.

Irresistible taglines pique curiosity, urging viewers to binge-watch seasons or readers to one-click "Buy" just to access the answers that only full immersion within your fictional worlds will satisfy. Study beloved show taglines, break down structural elements, then refine your own until conveying genre, stakes, time period, and aesthetic essence, proving undeniably compelling.

Expand loglines into longer pitches when engaging literary agents, publishers, and influencers. Map out additional layers of helpful detail and specificity while retaining intrigue - walk a fine line between necessary background expositions without excessive verbosity that diminishes intrinsic excitement. Edit ruthlessly, avoiding sluggish rambling. Every sentence must feel essential.

Social media platforms provide prolific avenues for directly engaging romance readership spheres and building anticipatory buzz for your upcoming releases. But avoid hard salesmanship that may turn off participation. Adopt an educational, thought leadership tonality, sharing glimpses into your creative process almost as if allowing privileged visibility into your workshop laboratory, experimenting with ideas blossoming into eventual manuscripts.

Curate compelling Pinterest boards capturing striking Wild West visuals that echo key themes in your novel. Pin images of landscapes, costumes, weapons - anything that helps transport viewers to the setting and time period.

Include short captions connecting each pin back to your story.

Start a YouTube or BookTube channel. Film creative vlogs from fictional locations, imagine episode recaps between chapters or act out dramatic scenes. Keep videos light-hearted, but give audiences a peek behind the curtain of your writing process.

Script Tiktok posts around big plot points or character reveals. Give Booktokers a space to discuss what's happened and speculate what's next. Be an active participant to build buzz and hype.

Search hashtags to find Bookstagram accounts run by fans of the Western romance genre. Reach out and send review copies to IG (Instagram) influencers, asking them to promote your book to their engaged followers.

Host giveaways for advanced review copies, also known as ARCs, or offer bookish merch like bookmarks and buttons. Drive traffic back to your website if you have one or an author page. Offer bonus scenes to superfans, cementing their loyalty.

Finally, don't forget to have fun! Authentically share your passion for Western romance. Creativity and enthusiasm are contagious - soon, readers will be your biggest promoters as you ride toward writing success together. Yee-haw!